THIS WALKER BOOK BELONGS TO:

_____ _____

_____ _____

_____ _____

First published 1989 by Hamish Hamilton Children's Books

This edition published 2013 by Walker Books Ltd
87 Vauxhall Walk, London SE11 5HJ

2 4 6 8 10 9 7 5 3 1

© 1989 Brun Ltd

The right of Anthony Browne to be identified as author/illustrator of this work
has been asserted by him in accordance with the Copyright, Designs and Patents Act 1988

This book has been typeset in New Century Schoolbook

Printed in China

British Library Cataloguing in Publication Data:
a catalogue record for this book is available from the British Library

ISBN 978-1-4063-4162-1

www.walker.co.uk

ANTHONY BROWNE

A
Bear-y
Tale

WALKER BOOKS
AND SUBSIDIARIES
LONDON · BOSTON · SYDNEY · AUCKLAND

Bear was walking in the forest.

"Hello, Wolf."

"Take a look at this."

"Hello, Giant."

"Here's a little something for you."

And Bear walked on.

"Hello, Witch."

"What's this?"

"Bye-bye, Witch."

"Hello, Bears."

"Feeling hungry?"

"Bye-bye, Bears."

Anthony Browne

Anthony Browne is one of the most celebrated author-illustrators of his generation. Acclaimed Children's Laureate from 2009 to 2011 and winner of multiple awards – including the prestigious Kate Greenaway Medal and the much coveted Hans Christian Andersen Award – Anthony is renowned for his unique style. His work is loved around the world.

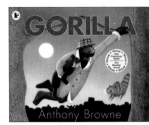
ISBN 978-1-4063-1327-7

ISBN 978-1-84428-559-4

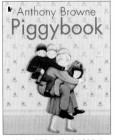
ISBN 978-1-4063-1328-4

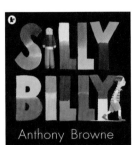
ISBN 978-1-4063-0576-0

ISBN 978-1-4063-1329-1

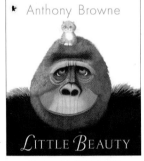
ISBN 978-1-4063-1930-9

ISBN 978-1-4063-1852-4

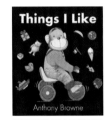
ISBN 978-0-7445-9858-2
ISBN 978-1-4063-2187-6
Board book edition

ISBN 978-1-4063-3851-5
ISBN 978-1-4063-4791-3
Board book edition

ISBN 978-0-7445-9857-5
ISBN 978-1-4063-2178-4
Board book edition

ISBN 978-1-4063-4533-9

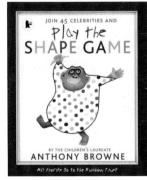
Willy the Wimp
ISBN 978-1-4063-1874-6

Willy the Champ
ISBN 978-1-4063-1873-9

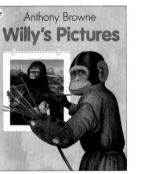
Willy's Pictures
ISBN 978-1-4063-1356-7

Willy the Dreamer
ISBN 978-1-4063-1357-4

ISBN 978-1-4063-2628-4

ISBN 978-1-4063-3131-8

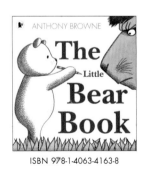
ISBN 978-1-4063-1339-0

ISBN 978-1-4063-4163-8

ISBN 978-1-4063-4164-5

ISBN 978-1-4063-2625-3

Available from all good booksellers

www.walker.co.uk